BABY BABOON

Other books by Mwenye Hadithi and Adrienne Kennaway

Greedy Zebra
Hot Hippo
Crafty Chameleon (winner of the Kate Greenaway Medal 1987)
Tricky Tortoise
Lazy Lion

British Library Cataloguing in Publication Data

A catalogue record for this book is available
from the British Library

ISBN 0 340 58048 8

First published 1993
First published in paperback 1994

Published by Hodder and Stoughton Children's Books,
a division of Hodder Headline plc,
338 Euston Road, NWI 3BH

Printed in Belgium by Proost International Book Production

BABY BABOON

by **Mwenye Hadithi**

Illustrated by **Adrienne Kennaway**

HODDER AND STOUGHTON
LONDON SYDNEY AUCKLAND

Baboon and Baby Baboon were playing in a leafy tree outside Leopard's cave.

Leopard was hungry, but he was also lazy.
So he lay silently in the tall, cool grass, with
just the tip of his tail showing.

Soon Hare came hop-hopping along.
Leopard leaped up from the long grass
and chased Hare. He chased him and
chased him, backwards and forwards . . .

. . . until Hare ran down a hole in the river-bank.

I've got you now, thought Leopard. And he hid
behind a big Yellowbark tree, waiting for Hare
to come out again.

He waited and waited.

Up in the tree, Baby Baboon laughed.
    Leopard grew thirsty and tired of waiting.
He called to Baboon and Baby Baboon:
    'I am going to the river for a drink. If you
will guard this hole for a moment, and make
sure Hare does not come out, I will share
my dinner with you.'

So Baboon came down and watched the hole. But while she watched, Hare ran to the end of the tunnel and dug his way out.

Leopard looked up just in time to see Hare
scampering away in the distance.
And up in the tree, Baby Baboon laughed
and laughed.

Leopard was very cross.

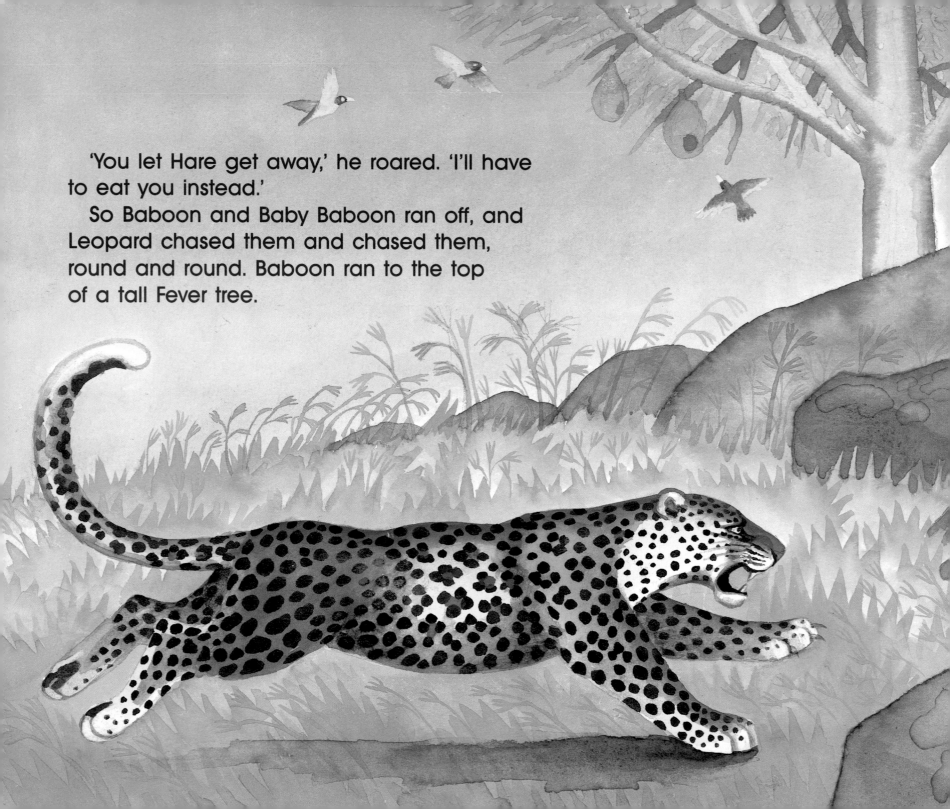

'You let Hare get away,' he roared. 'I'll have
to eat you instead.'

So Baboon and Baby Baboon ran off, and
Leopard chased them and chased them,
round and round. Baboon ran to the top
of a tall Fever tree.

But Baby Baboon ran too slowly, and Leopard
caught him firmly by the tail.
And Baby Baboon didn't laugh. Not once.
'Help, help,' he cried.

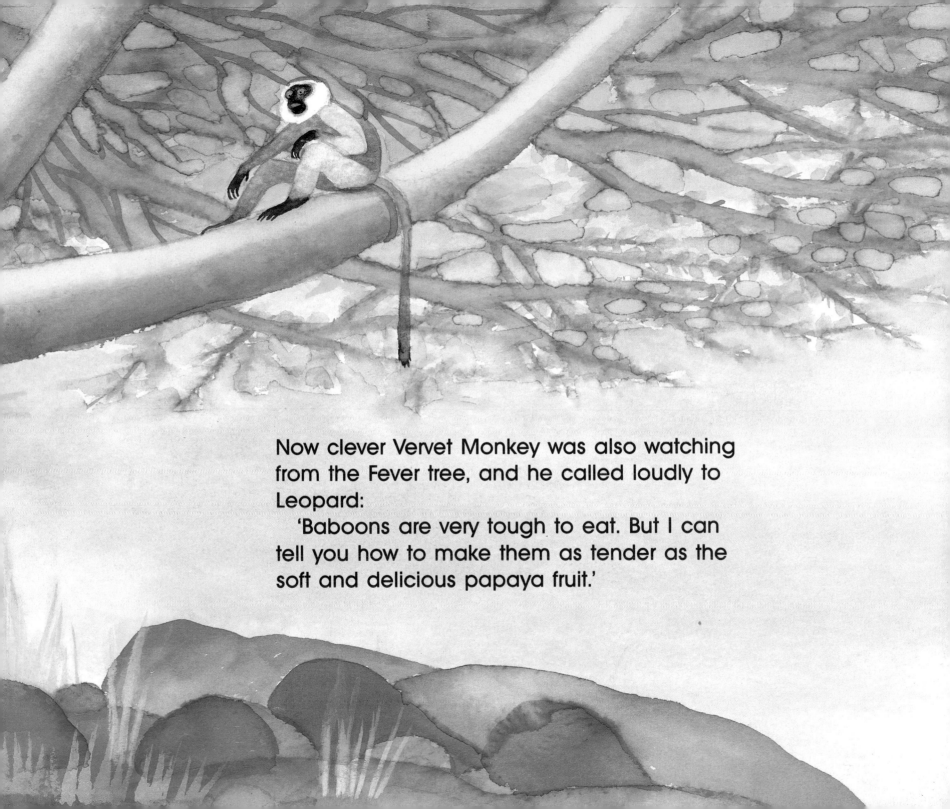

Now clever Vervet Monkey was also watching from the Fever tree, and he called loudly to Leopard:

'Baboons are very tough to eat. But I can tell you how to make them as tender as the soft and delicious papaya fruit.'

'How is that?' growled Leopard.

'You throw a baboon high-as-can-be in the air,' suggested Vervet Monkey. 'The more times the better. And soon the baboon will make a very tender, tasty snack.'

'Well, they are extremely tough to chew,' grunted Leopard. So he threw Baby Baboon high-as-can-be in the air and . . .

. . . just as he flew by, Baboon grabbed Baby
Baboon and they went swinging away through
the trees.

And Baby Baboon laughed and laughed.
And Leopard was crosser and hungrier than ever. He ran after them and chased them, up and down, but he couldn't catch them at all.

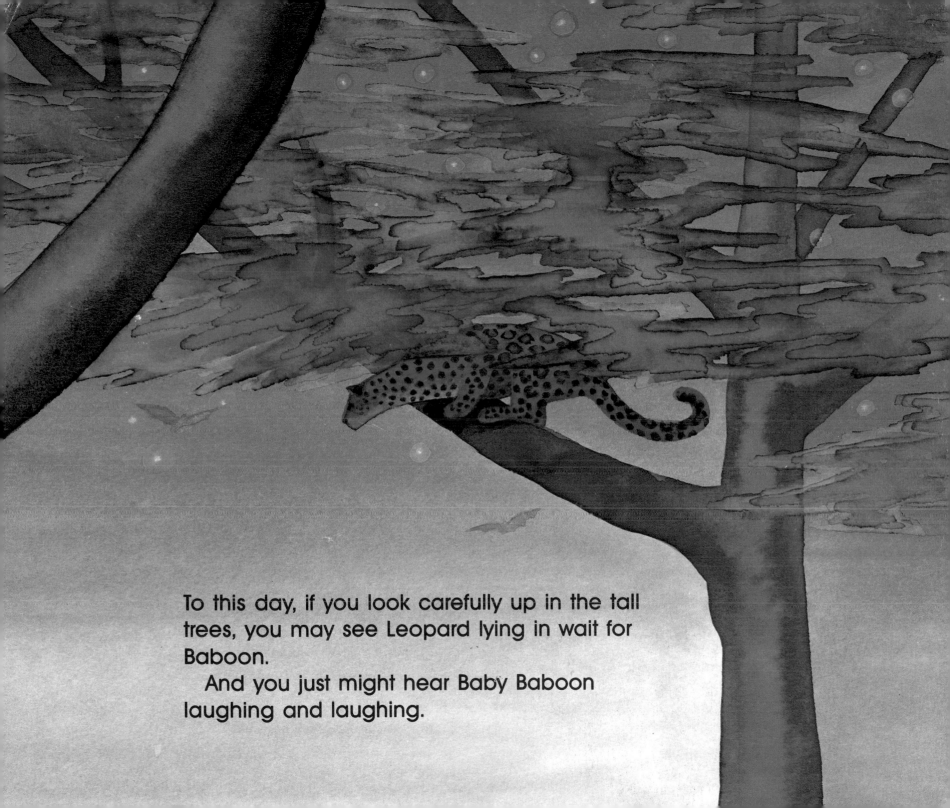

To this day, if you look carefully up in the tall trees, you may see Leopard lying in wait for Baboon.

And you just might hear Baby Baboon laughing and laughing.